CHRIS HIGGINS

TROUBLE NEXT DOOR

Bloomsbury Publishing, London, Oxford,
New York, New Delhi and Sydney

First published in Great Britain in January 2017
by Bloomsbury Publishing Plc
50 Bedford Square, London WC1B 3DP

www.bloomsbury.com

BLOOMSBURY is a registered trademark of
Bloomsbury Publishing Plc

A CIP catalogue record for this book is available
from the British Library

ISBN 978 1 4088 6883 6

MIX
Paper from
responsible sources
FSC® C020471
FSC
www.fsc.org

Printed and bound in Great Britain by
CPI Group (UK) Ltd, Croydon CR0 4YY

1 3 5 7 9 10 8 6 4 2

CHRIS
HIGGINS

TROUBLE
NEXT
DOOR

Illustrated by
Emily
MacKenzie

MOVING HOUSE

Bella thought the new house looked strange. She stood in the overgrown garden with scratchy grass up to her knees and stared at it with Sid.

Something was wrong.

"It's not a new house, it's an old house," she said.

"Yes," said Mum. "It's a very old cottage. It was built hundreds of years ago."

"But you said we were moving to a new house!"

"Oh dear!" Mum looked sorry. "I meant it was new to us."

"It's got a face," said Sid.

Her little brother was right. The house did have a face.

Its roof was a hat with a crooked chimney poking up from it like a feather, and its gutters, covered in moss, were untidy eyebrows. Beneath them two dark bedroom windows peeped out at them sleepily.

"It's pleased to see us," said Sid.

"Yes," smiled Mum. "It's glad a family's come to live in it again. It's been empty for a long time."

Sid liked the house but Bella wasn't sure. She'd thought she was moving to a nice new house in the countryside, by the sea.

This house looked like it was about to fall down.

And the countryside smelt of poo. Cow poo. The field in front of the house stank of it.

And there was no sign of the sea.

"Let's go inside and take a look," said Dad.

He took a key out of his pocket and turned the lock.

Slowly, the door opened with a loud creaking noise.

INSIDE THE COTTAGE

Inside, it was dark and dusty.

"I don't like it," said Bella. "It smells funny."

"It just needs a good airing," said Mum. "It's been shut up for a long time."

Bella looked around. It wasn't a proper house at all, just one big room with a low ceiling and black wooden beams running across it. There was a wooden door at the back leading to the kitchen, a huge fireplace and a staircase in the far corner.

Sid stuck his head up inside the fireplace. "Look at this, Bella! It's ENORMOUS!"

"*NORMOUS ... ORMOUS ... ORMOUS,*"
echoed the fireplace as soot dropped
down at their feet.

"Careful!" said Dad. "It probably
hasn't been swept for years."

Bella peered up the chimney. It
smelt of burning and was so dark
you couldn't see the top.

"In the olden days they'd
have sent kids like you up there
to clean it," remarked Dad.

"Wicked!" said Sid.

He shot upstairs to explore but
Bella hung back.

"What's up, sweetheart?"
Mum knelt down in front of
her and her face was kind and

soft. This made Bella feel worse.

"I want to go home," she whispered.

"I know, darling," said Mum gently. "But this is your home now. You're going to love living here."

"No I'm not. I hate it!" said Bella, which wasn't really true.

Mum gave a big sigh and got to her feet. "Come on!" she said, holding out her hand. "We'll go and choose your bedroom."

Upstairs was a landing leading to three bedrooms and a bathroom. A set of rickety old steps disappeared around a corner.

"What's up there?" asked Bella.

"The attic!" said Sid, appearing

beside her. "Let's take a look."

Bella shook her head. She didn't want to see a mouldy old attic. She wanted to choose her room.

The first bedroom was too big and bare.

The second was too small and cramped.

Bella sighed. She was *never* going to like it here.

"Let's take a look at the third bedroom," said Mum.

With a long face, Bella pushed the door open.

Bright yellow sunshine streamed across the polished floorboards. The window dropped almost down to the floor and it had a cushioned seat. Through it she could see the field opposite, the lane and into next door's front garden.

Bella's face lit up. "It's just right!"

Mum beamed. "I thought it would be. We should have called you Goldilocks."

Bella couldn't wait for night-time so she could go to sleep in her new bedroom.

BEDTIME

Bella lay in bed, clutching the duvet up to her neck.

Now it was bedtime, it wasn't sunny in her new bedroom any more. It was really dark. She'd never known it to be this dark before. Dad explained it was because there were no street lights.

"You'll be able to see the stars," he said, tucking her in.

When he went downstairs, she got out of bed and looked through the funny little low-down window. Dad was wrong. There were no stars tonight. There was no moon either. They were hiding behind a blanket of cloud.

Which meant it was pitch black. Inside and out.

"Bella?" called Dad. "What are you doing out of bed?"

"I'm not!" she fibbed, scurrying back before he caught her.

"Night, night," said Dad firmly, tucking her in for the second time.

As soon as he'd gone, Bella got back out again, switched the light on and

peered under the bed.

Then she looked in the wardrobe.

Then she poked
her head out of her
bedroom door

and stared at the rickety
old steps in the gloomy
corner of the landing.
The steps that led
up to the attic.

There was nothing there.

Phew! Bella breathed a big sigh of relief and got back into her lovely soft bed and snuggled down happily. Soon she could feel herself drifting off to sleep.

Mmm ... soft and squashy ... squishy-squashy ... fluttery-flappy ...

Fluttery-flappy? Bella raised her head. What was that sound? It was coming from the attic.

What sort of creature would flap around in the middle of the night frightening people?

Quick as a flash, the answer came to her. A GHOST!!!!!!!!!!!

"Mu-um!" she whimpered. But there was no answer.

"MU-UM!"

she called louder.

Footsteps stomped up the stairs and the light snapped on. "There's a ghost in our attic!" shrieked Bella. "I heard it flapping."

Mum sat on the bed and listened. "I can't hear anything. It's probably a bird. We'll look for it in the morning."

Bella could tell she didn't believe her. "Look for it *now*!"

"No. It's too dark." Mum tucked her in so tightly she could hardly breathe. "Now close your eyes and go to sleep!"

Bella lay still in the darkness, concentrating. She was sure she could still hear it up there, fluttering about.

She'd never get to sleep like this! Then she had a brainwave.

She wriggled out of her tight bed and tiptoed over to her case, which was waiting to be unpacked. Rummaging through it in the dark, Bella found just what she was

looking for. Her fluffy earmuffs

and her favourite woolly hat.

They should do the trick!

Bella jumped into bed and pulled her hat down over her ears, her earmuffs over her hat and her pillow over her head.

Then she listened as hard as she could.

Nothing!

At last, Bella fell fast asleep.

A NICE SURPRISE

Bella was sitting on the front doorstep feeling grumpy.

It wasn't fair. She'd told Sid there was a ghost in their attic and he wanted to see it. But Mum said there was nothing there and they should go out to play, even though she'd *promised* they would look for it in the morning.

Mum and Dad were really busy. Dad was laying a new carpet in the living room and Mum was scrubbing and polishing every available surface.

Bella was bored. It was all right for Sid. He was happy poking a stick around in the earth but Bella didn't know what to do. She wished she had someone to play with.

"Hello," said a voice, and she looked around. There was no one to be seen. "Hell-o-o!" persisted the voice. "I'm here!"

Bella and
Sid sprang to
their feet. The voice
seemed to be coming
from the cottage next door.
But when they peered over the wall
there was nobody there. Just a messy
garden with a jumble of wild flowers
and grass and a big, sprawling tree,
thick with leaves.

"Look up!"
commanded the voice.
It was coming from
high up in the tree.

Two bare legs
appeared,
then a pair of dusty
pink shorts,

a rather grubby
white T-shirt with a
mermaid on it and,
finally, a head.
A girl dangled
from a branch for
a second, arms
outstretched,

then she raised her legs and started swinging, higher and higher. Suddenly, she launched herself into the air, did a backward somersault and landed the right way up, arms straight, like a gymnast.

"Wow!" said Bella.

"Wow!" said Sid.

"Hello," she repeated, dusting herself down. "I'm Magda."

"I'm Bella and this is Sid," replied Bella. Then she remembered her manners. "How do you do?"

"How do I do what?" asked Magda. Her voice sounded different.

"That's what you say to be polite," said Bella.

The children examined each other curiously.

Bella thought that she would like to have long fair plaits and bright blue eyes like Magda.

"I like your plaits," she said.

"I like your curls," replied Magda. "And his." She pointed to Sid.

Sid grinned at Magda. "I'm five," he said. "How old are you?"

"Eight."

"I'm eight too," said Bella, pleased.

"Twins!" said Magda, and Bella was even more pleased.

"Do you live here?" she asked.

"I do now," said Magda. "I used to live in Poland."

"Where's that?"

Magda shrugged. "A long way away."

"I used to live a long way away too," said Bella sadly. "I don't know anybody here."

"You know me," said Magda. "Can I come and play in your back garden? It's got raspberries in it."

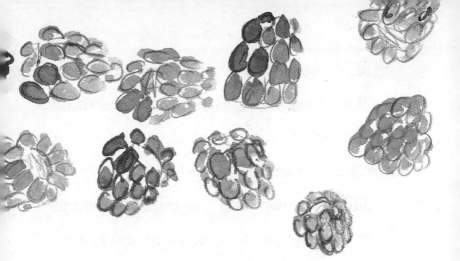

RASPBERRIES
AND RHUBARB

Bella and Sid hadn't been in their back garden yet. They went out of their front gate and followed Magda around to the back.

Their garden was huge and very untidy! Magda knew all about it.

She showed them where the raspberries

were growing wild on tall, thin stems.

"Mmmm," she said, popping one into her mouth. And another. And another. Then she said generously, "Help yourselves."

Bella picked a big fat one and bit into it. It burst on her tongue in an explosion of juice.

"I never knew raspberries grew in gardens," mumbled Sid, cramming them into his mouth as fast as he could. "I thought you bought them in a shop for a special treat."

"You're funny!" laughed Magda and Sid laughed too but Bella knew he wasn't joking.

"You've got blackberries as well," said Magda.

"Where?" Sid couldn't believe his luck.

"Over there." Magda pointed to the hedge. "But they won't be ready till the end of summer. Here's some rhubarb. That's ready to eat now."

Magda pointed to some flat, green leaves. Bella snapped one off and felt its rubbery surface.

"Just the stalks, not the leaves," warned Magda. "They're poisonous."

Bella dropped the rhubarb leaf in horror and rubbed her hand on her jeans, trying to get rid of the poison.

"They can't hurt you if you touch them. Only if you eat them," explained Magda, who seemed to know everything.

They picked some more raspberries and sat down to eat them. Soon their hands and faces were stained bright red with raspberry juice.

"Our house is really old," said Bella, gazing up at it.

"I know," said Magda. "Mine is too."

"Our house has got a GINORMOUS fireplace," said Sid, stretching his arms as wide as he could.

"Can I see it?" asked Magda.

"OK," said Sid, and led the way proudly into the house.

JUST LIKE HOME

Inside, there was a nice surprise. Dad had finished laying the new carpet, which was a lovely soft pink, Bella's favourite colour. Mum had finished polishing and all the furniture was in place. Even the television was plugged in ready for action, and the books and ornaments were neatly arranged on the shelves.

"What do you think?" asked Mum.

Mum and Dad looked hot and tired after all their hard work but very pleased with themselves.

"It's just like home!" cried Bella.

"Only cleaner and tidier," said Sid.

Mum smiled. "Who's this?"

"Magda. She lives next door. Can I put my shorts on?" said Bella, who wanted to be exactly like her new friend.

"When we've unpacked them," said Mum. "Magda, does your mother know you're here?"

"She's at work," explained Magda. "Babcia's looking after me."

"Who's Bahp-cha?" asked Bella, because that's what it sounded like.

"Grandma."

"Does she know where you are?" asked Mum.

Magda shrugged. "I guess. I often come here to play. In the garden, I mean. Because of the raspberries."

"Tell you what," said Mum. "I could do with a nice cup of tea after all our hard work. I'll ask her to join us. Then we can all get to know each other properly."

"Good idea," said Dad. "I'll put the kettle on." And he went off to the kitchen to make the tea.

"Won't be long," said Mum, looking excited at the thought of making friends with the neighbours. "Bella, you're in charge!"

Bella drew herself up to her full height as Mum, with one more satisfied look around her sparkling new room, disappeared out of the front door.

EXPLORING

Bella liked being left in charge. It made her feel grown up and responsible.

"Look at our fireplace," said Sid. "Isn't it enormous?"

"Wow! It's much bigger than ours!" said Magda, and Sid and Bella grinned proudly.

Magda ran over and stuck her head up inside it.

"Hello-o!" she shouted, and the echo shouted back, "*Hello-o … o … o!*"

Tiny particles of soot fell into the grate.

Sid stuck his head up too. "I can see you!" he bellowed.

"*See you … you … ou!*" bounced back his voice, and Magda and Sid burst out laughing. Their laughter rang back and this made them laugh even louder.

More soot fell down the chimney.

"Careful!" warned Bella, but they weren't listening. Magda had spotted something.

"Look!" she said. "There's a little ledge up there. I wonder what it's for."

"Climbing," said Sid. "My dad said they used to send kids like us up the chimneys to clean them in the olden days."

"Awesome!" said Magda and before Bella could stop her, she'd put her foot on the ledge and hauled herself up into the chimney.

"Magda!" cried Bella in alarm. "What are you doing?"

"Climbing up to the top!" she called back. "It's easy. There are little footholds. Oops! Missed one!"

A rush of soot fell down on to

Sid's face. Bella tried to clean him up with her sleeve. She could hear Magda coughing inside the chimney.

"It's stinky up here," she complained.

"Come on down then!" yelled Bella.

"I can't!" said Magda, her voice muffled. "I'm stuck!"

Outside Bella could hear voices. Oh no! Her mum was coming up the garden path with Magda's grandma.

Sid's face was still smudged with black and there was a smattering of soot on the new carpet. Quickly, Bella rubbed it with her toe but only made it worse.

Mum would go bananas if she caught Magda up the chimney!

Bella peered up anxiously and could just make out Magda's foot.

"Magda! Come down this minute!"

"I'm trying!" said Magda. "I think if I wriggle about a bit I might be able to get myself loose ..."

From inside the chimney Bella could hear Magda twisting and grunting as she tried to free herself.

Suddenly, she gave an almighty yell and tumbled down, landing with a thud on her bottom. She sat up immediately, coughing and spluttering, black from head to toe.

And then, just as though someone had turned on a tap, soot poured down the chimney. Bella and Sid jumped back in horror as it bounced off the hearth and

"BELL

billowed around the room like smoke, filling the air with black, choking fumes.

Mum opened the front door and gazed with horror at her once spotless new room, now swirling with soot.

"What on earth?" she asked in a high, squeaky voice.

And then she opened her mouth wide and roared,

AAAA!"

BABCIA TO
THE RESCUE

Thank goodness for Babcia, that's all Bella could think.

Babcia was round and wrinkled like an old apple. She looked like a sweet old lady but looks can be deceptive.

In the war against dirt, Babcia was a general with many successful military campaigns under her belt. An invasion of soot was nothing to her.

Unlike Mum, who was screeching a lot but not actually doing anything, and Dad, who was scratching his head and staring bemused at his blackened living room, Babcia immediately sprang into action. First she hauled her granddaughter to her feet by the elbow and took her outside to hose her down.

Then she came back with a damp, deflated Magda and an arsenal of weapons.

These included:

a mop and bucket,

a scrubbing brush,

a broom,

a dustpan and brush,

spray polish,

dusters

and an old vacuum cleaner as big as a tank.

Babcia threw open the windows and doors and led the others into battle.

She flung the rugs over the washing line and ordered Dad to beat the living daylights out of them.

She pegged out the cushions and told Sid to whack them hard with the broom.

She instructed Bella to dust the books
within an inch of their lives.

She commanded Magda
to wipe the ornaments
clean carefully.

She put Mum in charge of brushing down the sofas and Dad (when he'd finished beating the rugs) in charge of washing down the walls.

Meanwhile Babcia scrubbed the fireplace, swabbed the mantelpiece,

scoured the skirting boards, polished the TV, buffed the bookshelves, mopped the coffee table, blitzed the carpet with the vacuum cleaner and blasted the final traces of soot from its hiding places.

Soon Magda grew bored with wiping ornaments carefully. She wanted to dust the books within an inch of their lives instead.

"Swap?" she asked Bella.

"OK," said Bella, though she couldn't help noticing that the ornaments Magda had already wiped were still a bit soot-smeared. She decided to go over them again.

"Careful with my best jug, Bella," warned Mum as Bella picked it up.

Bella bit her lip. She'd spotted a crack in it. Magda must have done it.

Mum had yelled at Bella when she'd discovered the living room was full of soot. Now she might blame her for cracking her best jug.

Should she tell Mum it was Magda's fault? Better not. She probably wouldn't notice. Anyway, you don't get your friends into trouble, do you?

Bella realised she already thought of Magda as a friend. It gave her a nice warm feeling inside.

TIME FOR
A BREAK

At last they were all finished.

Everyone stood and stared at the living room.

"Nice carpet," remarked Babcia. "Grey is a good colour, yes?"

"It was pink," said Mum faintly.

"How about that cup of tea?" suggested Dad.

"I'll make it!" offered Magda, and dashed off to the kitchen.

"What a thoughtful child!" said Mum, sinking down thankfully on to the sofa beside Babcia. "You've both been so helpful. I don't know how we'd have managed without you."

Bella tried to work out how Magda had emerged as the hero in all this but it was too complicated, so she followed her new friend out to the kitchen instead and Sid trailed after her.

The kitchen was full of steam and Magda was doing a handstand against the back door.

Bella switched off the kettle, filled the teapot and looked around for mugs. Most things were still in packing cases.

"There are some pretty cups in that

box," said upside-down Magda, her plaits hanging down to the floor.

"Oh!" said Bella, looking at the dainty cups and saucers in the box on the worktop. "They're my mum's best tea service. They were a wedding present. We only use them for special occasions."

"This is a special occasion," said Magda.

"It's the day we became best friends."

Bella got that nice warm feeling again. She hadn't realised they were *best* friends.

"Shall I put some plates out too?" said Magda. "Then we can have some biscuits."

"Good idea," said Bella.

Magda swung her legs over, somersaulted across the room and caught the edge of the box with her foot.

There was an ominous crunch and a tinkling noise.

"Oops! Sorry!" said Magda, peering into the box. "Don't worry, it's only one or two. There's plenty more."

"I'll get the biscuits!" said Sid and he stood on a chair to open the cupboard. "We've got rich tea, custard creams, Jammie Dodgers and chocolate digestives. Which ones do you want?"

"All of them," said Magda, opening the packets.

Bella thought she should stop her but she didn't know how to. Instead she carefully laid out cups, saucers and plates on a tray with milk and sugar, just like she'd seen Mum do. Then she poured the tea and arranged a selection of biscuits nicely on a plate.

"That's not enough!" said Magda, and emptied the rest on top. Some fell on the floor and broke.

"Never mind," said Magda, gobbling up the broken bits. "I'll take in the tray of tea."

"And I'll take in the biscuits," said Sid.

Magda led the way into the living room and offered the tea to Mum.

"Oh, what a good girl you are, Magda," said Mum, helping herself to a cup. "You've set this out so nicely."

Bella waited for Magda to say that actually it was Bella who had set it out nicely but she seemed to have forgotten.

Bella felt a teeny bit annoyed.

Mum's eyes opened very wide when she saw the plate piled high with biscuits, but because they had guests all she said was, "Goodness me, who arranged those?"

"Bella," said Magda and helped herself to a chocolate digestive.

And a Jammie Dodger.

Plus two more chocolate digestives and a custard cream.

THINKING
IT OVER

When Babcia and Magda left, Mum had a great deal to say about too many biscuits, broken tea sets, cracked favourite jugs, climbing up chimneys and sooty living rooms.

All of which, for some reason, she seemed to think was Bella's fault. Bella tried to explain but Mum refused to listen.

"You have to take your share of the responsibility," she said sternly. "Now go to your room and reflect upon your actions." (Mum always spoke in long words when she was cross.)

Bella went upstairs and lay down on her bed and did as she was told. But, try as hard as she could, the more she reflected the less she understood how *her* actions had led to the chain of events.

It was a mystery.

It seemed to her that it was Magda who'd caused the trouble but *she* who'd got the blame. That wasn't fair, was it?

Above her head came a soft, fluttering noise and Bella sat bolt upright. Oh no! The ghost was back!

"Mum!" she said automatically.

Then Bella thought that, at this precise moment, the ghost was probably less scary than her mum, so she decided to cover her ears and sing loudly to drown out the noise. Six songs later, it had stopped. Bella got up and knelt down by her bedroom window to take her mind off what might be up there in the attic.

In next door's garden Magda was

practising her cartwheels. She was very
good at them.

Magda looked up and spotted Bella
watching her. She waved and Bella waved
back.

Magda put her fingers into the corners of
her mouth and waggled her tongue. Bella
giggled and pulled a funny face back.

Magda hung her arms down to the ground and leapt around the garden whooping and pretending to be a monkey. Bella laughed out loud and did the same thing around her bedroom even though Magda couldn't see her.

Then Bella waggled her ears at Magda, and Magda waggled her plaits back at Bella.

They kept on playing, taking it in turns to do silly things and copy each other, until Mum called Bella down for lunch.

"Can I play with Magda this afternoon?" asked Bella through a mouthful of baked beans. She was so much fun, she'd forgotten she'd ever been cross with her.

"No," said Mum.

"Tomorrow?" said Bella hopefully.

"We'll see," said Mum.

Bella sighed. "We'll see" was Mum-speak for: "*Don't ask again and hopefully you'll forget all about it.*"

She wouldn't forget though. She wanted Magda to teach her how to do proper cartwheels. And handstands.

It was nice having a best friend next door.

NOTHING
TO DO

To Bella's disappointment, the next morning it was pouring with rain.

After breakfast Bella and Sid knelt on the window seat and traced the raindrops streaking down the windowpane, first with their fingers, then with their noses. Then Sid got silly and did it with his tongue and Mum asked Bella to read him a book.

Bella read Sid's favourite story. Over and over again.

Then she asked if they could go up to the attic to look for the ghost. But Mum said no, she was too busy and there wasn't one. Bella and Sid watched television. Lots.

Mum and Dad seemed to have forgotten all about them.

Bella discovered an interesting fact. The longer you watch television the harder it is to sit upright. When Mum walked in to see what they were up to, Bella was slumped sideways and Sid was sprawled across her on the sofa.

Mum switched the television off.

"That's enough. You'll get square eyes," she said, which was not true because

Great-Grandma, who was very old, watched television all day long and her eyes were still round.

But Bella had discovered another interesting fact. Watching too much television was like eating too much food. You get sick of it in the end.

"Go and sort your bedrooms out," said

Mum. "Bella, you need to unpack."

Sid scampered upstairs and Bella tore up behind him. When she went into her bedroom, she paused to listen for the ghost but all she could hear was the sound of rain pattering on the roof.

First she made her bed. Then she started to hang her clothes up.

It was quite tricky because they kept sliding off the hangers, so Bella turned her attention to her big box of books instead. She loved reading. She had more books than anyone else she knew.

Bella decided to arrange them by author alphabetically, like they did in the library. That way she would always be able to lay her hands quickly on the one that she wanted.

Her books were better behaved than her clothes. Bella, who liked arranging things neatly, hummed to herself as she filled her bookcase and the shelves beside her bed with books in the right order. It took a long time but it was worth it.

Bella put the last book in place and

sighed happily. That was a job well done. Now all she had to do was to finish hanging her clothes up properly and then Mum would be really pleased with her.

Rat-a-tat-tat!

Someone was at the front door.

MANY HANDS

Bella looked out of the window.

It was Magda!

Bella raced downstairs and flung open
the door.

"Coming out to play?" asked Magda,
looking a bit damp.

"It's raining."

"Oh yes. I'd better come in then,"

Magda said and stepped inside the house.

"Who's that?" asked Mum, poking her head around the kitchen door. "Oh, it's you, Magda. Bella's busy tidying her bedroom."

"Can I help?" asked Magda. "I'm good at tidying."

Mum hesitated and then she smiled. "That's very kind of you, Magda. You'd better tell your grandma where you are though."

"She already knows," said Magda. "Come on, Bella." She led the way upstairs.

"Wow!" she said, when she walked into Bella's bedroom. "This is soooooo neat and tidy."

Bella was pleased. "I know. I've just put all my books into alphabetical order."

"That's boring," said Magda, bouncing up and down happily on Bella's newly made bed. "Everyone does that. Why don't you sort them a different way?"

"How?" asked Bella, puzzled.

"Put them face out, that's what I do. Then you can see the covers. Watch me do a headstand!"

Magda put her head on Bella's pillow and flung her legs up, crashing into the shelf above, where Bella kept her special things.

Somehow Bella managed to catch her tiny house made of seashells and luckily the glass clown Grandma had brought her back from Italy fell safely on to the bed. But her garden-in-a-shoebox, which won second prize in the Spring Show, went flying, scattering soil and plants everywhere, and so did her jewellery box and all its contents.

"Sorreeeee!" said Magda.

"Quick! Let's clean it up before Mum sees it!" said Bella in alarm.

"No, let's organise your books first!" said Magda and she began to grab them off the shelves.

Very soon the bookcase and shelves were full but there were still lots of books left over.

"That didn't work," said Bella. "They take up too much room that way."

"It's your fault," explained Magda. "You've got too many books. Tell you what! I'll take these home with me."

She started picking up the rest of the books.

"No," said Bella quickly, snatching them back. "Let's arrange them a different way. How about size?"

"Oh!" said Magda, disappointed. "That's boring too." Then she brightened up. "I know! We could colour-code them. Put all the blues together and all the pinks and so on. That would be really cool."

"I don't know …" said Bella doubtfully. It sounded like a good suggestion but she was beginning to learn that when Magda lent a hand things did not always go according to plan.

But it was too late. Magda was already sweeping the books on to the bedroom floor. "Don't worry, I'll help you."

"So will I," said Sid, appearing from nowhere. "Hello, Magda!"

TOO MANY
COOKS

Magda and Sid were really good at taking the books down from the shelves but not so good at putting them back up again. The pile on the floor seemed to be growing.

Colour-coding turned out to be a much

harder job than Bella thought it would be. Magda had quite different ideas from her about which book was what shade and kept swapping them around.

After a while Magda got bored and peered inside Bella's case. "Look at all your clothes! Would you like me to hang them up for you?"

"Yes please!" said Bella gratefully.

She picked up Bella's party dress. "This is nice. Can I try it on?"

"Help yourself," said Bella, so Magda did.

Then she dropped it on the floor and tried on Bella's new top and leggings.

Then she tried on all the rest of her clothes as well and forgot all about hanging them up.

"Shall we tidy up now?" said Bella worriedly, eyeing the messy bed, the piles of books, the mounds of clothes, the scattered jewellery and the clumps of soil and plants.

"In a minute. Let's play fashion shows first," said Magda. "We need high-heeled shoes. Has your mum got some?"

That sounded like fun. Bella ran off to fetch them from her mum's room. Magda came too and helped herself to the highest pair she could find. Suddenly her eyes lit up. She'd spotted Mum's wedding dress hanging in the wardrobe.

"I've changed my mind. Let's play weddings instead! I'll be the bride."

Magda was full of good ideas. All the same, Bella felt a bit nervous.

"I don't think Mum would like you wearing her wedding dress."

"She won't know," said Magda. "We'll just have one game and then I'll put it back. Sid, you can be the bridegroom."

Sid jumped up and down with excitement but Bella still wasn't sure.

"Tell you what," said Magda. "You be the bride and I'll be the vicar. Your mum won't mind you trying on her wedding dress. My mum says I can wear hers when I get married."

"OK," said Bella, happily. Magda was so kind.

They dressed Sid up in a pair of Dad's

trousers but they fell down round his ankles, so instead he wore his favourite Superman pyjamas with a jacket of Dad's that came down to the floor.

"This is fun," giggled Bella, holding the hem up off the floor and managing a rather precarious twirl in Mum's tall shoes. "I feel beautiful."

"You look beautiful, Bella," said Sid. "I'm glad I'm marrying you."

"Now we are ready to start. We will all sing together, '*Here Comes the Bride*'," instructed Magda in a vicar's voice. "It goes like this.

Dee, dee dee dee

Dee, dee dee dee …

Oops! I nearly forgot!" She clapped her hand to her mouth. "You need a bouquet,

Bella. Go and pick some flowers from my garden."

Bella wobbled downstairs on her high heels, out of her garden and into Magda's. It was still raining and very muddy but she managed to pick some nice flowers even though she got a bit wet.

"What on earth … !" said Mum as she caught sight of a small, damp, wobbly bride disappearing back upstairs. She dashed up after her, just in time to see the bride trip head over heels across the pile of books and clothes on the floor of a very messy bedroom and put her high spiky heel through her beautiful but rather muddy wedding dress.

IN THE DOGHOUSE

"You're in the doghouse, Bella," Dad whispered to her when he looked in on her mid-afternoon. He'd tiptoed in with his finger to his lips, handed her a rocket lolly from the freezer and tiptoed back out again.

She wasn't literally in the doghouse. That would mean she was in a kennel.

Though she might as well be.

She was in her bedroom on her own, reflecting on her actions. Again. Being in the doghouse meant she was in BIG TROUBLE!

She'd tried to explain to Mum that it wasn't her fault, it was an accident, but Mum wouldn't listen.

"I'm very disappointed in you, Bella," she'd said. "You used to be such a good girl. Now go to your room and don't come down till I tell you."

At tea time Mum allowed Bella downstairs to eat fish and chips, her favourite, but she didn't enjoy them very much. Not with the torn, muddy wedding dress hanging on the back of the door like a phantom bride, reminding her of her misdeeds.

"I'm going to have to take it to a specialist shop to put it right and it's going to cost a fortune!" complained Mum for the umpteenth time.

"Is it worth it?" asked Dad, who was far more interested in tucking into his cod and chips.

"I mean, it's not like you're ever going to wear it again, is it? You probably wouldn't fit into it now, even if you wanted to."

The room fell silent but Dad didn't notice. He was too busy shoving forkfuls of food into his mouth.

Mum's face grew redder and redder. Bella held her breath, waiting for her to go *bang*.

When she did, it was in a surprisingly quiet way, like a controlled explosion. She pushed her plate away, stood up quietly, picked up Dad's dinner and chucked it in the bin, plate and all. Then she sat back down again at the table, with her arms folded and her nose in the air.

Dad looked really funny sitting there with his knife and fork in his hands and no dinner. He pretended to look for it under the table and under his chair and Sid started laughing. Mum ignored him.

Dad got up and looked for his dinner behind the curtain.

Bella giggled. She couldn't help it.

Then he looked behind the cushions.

Mum took no notice. But Bella noticed her shoulders were shaking.

Dad scratched his head, bent down with his hands on his knees and peered up the chimney.

Sid and Bella yelped with laughter but Mum bit her lip and kept her mouth straight. She couldn't stop her eyes from smiling though.

Finally, Dad got down on his tummy and crawled under the coffee table. He lay there with his head on his hands, blinking at them sadly.

"What are you doing, Dad?" asked Bella.

"Woof," he said. "I'm in the doghouse."

Everyone burst out laughing.

Even Mum.

GOOD
INTENTIONS

The next morning, just as they were finishing breakfast, Magda knocked on the door. She was wearing a short frilly skirt and a pretty top, and she had blue ribbons in her hair which fanned out over her shoulders. Bella thought that she looked like an angel. All she needed was a pair of wings.

She looked a bit nervous when she saw Mum standing behind Bella.

"Please can Bella and Sid come out to play?" she asked in a timid little voice, and Bella thought she even sounded like an angel.

Mum must have thought so too because she said, "All right, as long as you promise to keep our Bella out of trouble."

"I will!" smiled Magda.

Bella and Sid ran out quickly before Mum could change her mind and followed Magda into her garden. Magda climbed up the tree so the others climbed up after her.

"I'm sorry you got told off about the wedding dress," said Magda.

"It doesn't matter," said Bella, and it didn't any more.

Magda pulled a half-eaten packet of sweets out of her pocket and handed them down to her.

"These are for you."

"Thank you," said Bella.

"That's all right, I don't like them. What shall we do today?"

Bella thought she'd like to sit in the tree and share her sweets with Sid. But Magda had other ideas.

"I know! Let's play Buried Alive."

"How d'you play that?"

"There's been a massive earthquake, right? You two have been buried alive and I'm the brave heroine who has to dig you out with my bare hands."

"Wicked!" said Sid, but Bella didn't want to be buried alive.

"No, let's play something else."

"OK, let's play Lost at Sea."

"How do you play Lost at Sea?"

"Two of us are sailors cast adrift in the ocean and one of us is a bloodthirsty pirate who rescues them then makes them walk the plank!"

"Yeah!" said Sid, his eyes shining. "I'm the bloodthirsty pirate!"

"No, *I'm* the bloodthirsty pirate," said Magda.

"Ohh!" said Sid, disappointed. "I don't want to play any more."

Magda looked fed up.

"Let's play school instead," suggested Bella.

Magda brightened up. "OK. I'm the teacher and you're in my class. You have to do what I tell you to."

Bella didn't like the sound of this. Neither did Sid.

"I know! Let's play hide-and-seek," he suggested.

"Where?"

"In your house."

"No, let's play it in your house," said Magda. "It's bigger than mine. There are more places to hide."

"Like the attic," piped up Sid.

"Have you got an attic? Luck-y!"

"Bella says there's a ghost in it," he

announced importantly.

Magda's jaw dropped open. "What? A real live one?"

"I'm not sure," said Bella. "Are ghosts alive or dead?"

"Does it go, *Whoo-whoo-whoooooo*?" Magda put her arms above her head,

wailing, and nearly fell head first out of the tree.

"No. But it flaps about a bit."

"It sounds like it's alive," said Magda. "Come on!"

She swung herself off the branch and dropped to the ground. The others scrambled down after her.

"Where are we going?" asked Sid.

"Your house. To find the ghost!"

"No, Magda!" yelled Bella, but her friend ignored her.

"Wait for us!" shouted Sid.

GHOST HUNT

"*Magda! Come back!*"

Too late! Magda was already knocking on the front door by the time Bella and Sid caught up with her.

"Stop it, Magda," said Bella, worriedly. "We're not allowed to play inside today. Not after yesterday."

"I don't want to *play*. I want to find

your ghost," Magda said and banged on the door again.

"No! Let's go back to your garden," said Bella, tugging at her arm, but Magda shook her off.

"Bella! I'm trying to help you! I'm going to scare your ghost away." She peered in through the window. "That's funny. There's nobody in."

"Where's Mum and Dad?" said Bella, puzzled.

"In the garage?" suggested Sid. "I heard them say they were going to clear it out this morning."

They tiptoed round the back and peeped inside the garage. Sure enough, Mum and Dad were both in there, knee-deep in boxes.

"Now's our chance," whispered Magda.

"Let's go and find the ghost while they're busy out here."

"*Please*, Bella?" pleaded Sid, his face bright with excitement.

Bella hesitated. She didn't want to get into trouble again. Though it wouldn't hurt to have a sneaky little peek in the attic, would it? Just to check there was nothing there. At least then she wouldn't have to worry that her house was haunted.

But ... "What if we do find a ghost up there?" she said in a tiny little voice.

Magda folded her arms and looked fierce like a warrior. "I'll chase it away for you!"

She would too. Magda was tough and brave and scared of nothing. If anyone could frighten a ghost off, it would be Magda.

Bella came to a decision.

"Come on then, quick!" she announced, more bravely than she actually felt. "Let's do it now."

IN THE ATTIC

The three children stared glumly at the old wooden door. It was locked.

Secretly, Bella was relieved.

"Have you got the key?" asked Magda.

"No," said Bella quickly.

"I can open it!" said Sid. He put his shoulder to the door and groaned,

"Heave!" but he was too little.

Magda refused to be beaten.

"Stand back!" she ordered. "I've seen them do this on TV."

Magda gave a massive kick. The door burst open and she fell into the attic. Clouds of dust rose up in the air.

From inside Bella thought she could hear a fluttering noise and her tummy turned a somersault.

Then she heard her mother's voice calling, "Bella? Sid? Where are you?" and her tummy did a backflip.

Mum would go mad if she caught them up here.

Quick as a flash, she pushed Sid into the dark void of the attic, stepped in after him and let the door fall shut behind them.

Inside it was pitch-black. Bella couldn't see a thing.

"Magda? Where are you?"

"Over here," shrieked Magda. "Something trailed across my face!"

"What?"

"I don't know!"

"It's the ghost!" breathed Sid. "Wicked!"

"Put the light on!" said Magda, sounding a bit agitated.

"There isn't one," said Bella.

"I'm getting out of here!" Magda pushed past her. "Where's the door?"

"Careful! Watch where you're going."

Now her eyes were adjusting, Bella discovered it wasn't pitch-black in the attic after all.

Above her head, sunshine sneaked through a narrow gap between the roof and the wall. A tiny shaft of light filtered across the middle of the room, leaving the rest in deep shadow.

Slowly she turned around.

The attic was empty. There was nothing here at all. Just billions of cobwebs hanging from the rafters like curtains, and a thick layer of dust.

"Cobwebs," she said. "That's what you felt."

Magda looked a bit sheepish.

Bella felt the floor give a little beneath her foot and wondered how safe it was.

"Stand on those beams," she warned her little brother. "Don't walk on the soft bits in between."

Sid did as he was told. "Where's the ghost?"

"Gone," said Magda, sounding more like her normal confident self. "I must have frightened it away." She stared around the attic with interest. "You know what? This would make a brilliant den for us."

Why didn't I think of that? thought Bella. *Magda always has the best ideas.*

"Come on, you two," said Bella." We'd better go down before Mum catches us."

But some things are easier said than done.

Too late, Bella realised that there was no handle on this side of the door.

It was shut tight and there was no way out.

THE GHOST

"We're trapped!" said Magda, sounding panicky again. "It's your fault, Bella!"

"There must be something we can do," said Bella desperately.

"I know! We could tie sheets together and climb out of the window," suggested Sid.

"We haven't got any sheets," said Magda. "And there's no window."

"We could ring 999 and call the fire brigade," he said.

"We haven't got a phone," she pointed out.

"We could cut down a huge tree and make a battering ram and bash the door down." Sid wasn't going to give up easily.

"Duh!" Magda spread her arms wide. "Show me the trees?"

Sid sat down on the beam to think up some more ideas.

Magda kicked the door but it wouldn't budge. "Right," she said, "we're going to have to call for help!"

"No!" said Bella in alarm. She didn't want her mum to know what they were up to. But it was too late.

"HELP!" shouted Magda, thumping the door with her fists.

Bella's heart sank. Now she was for it.

Then she heard something. A soft, whispering, fluttering sound. It was coming from above.

Bella looked up. She couldn't see anything but she knew. Something was up there in the shadows, watching them.

Then she heard it again. Quiet but spooky, it made the hairs on Bella's neck stand on end. She sat down next to Sid and put her arm around him.

"Is that the ghost?" whispered Sid, shuffling up close to her.

But before Bella could answer, Magda bawled, "HEEEEEEELP!" at the top of her voice.

And that's when it happened.

Out of the dark, with a flurry of wings and a blood-curdling shriek, the ghost came swooping down from the rafters and made straight for Magda.

Magda screeched and ducked as it skimmed her head, swept back up into the roof then dropped down again.

Magda fell to her knees and kept on screeching. The crazy, flapping thing kept coming at her, whirling and wheeling, diving and squealing. The more she screamed, the closer it came and the faster it flew.

Bella leapt to her feet to save her friend. She would beat off the ghost with her own bare hands if she had to.

There was a loud crack as her foot went through the floor.

"Watch out!" Sid yelled and tried to grab her. But it was too late.

With an almighty crash, the floor gave way and Bella felt herself falling.

The others watched in horror as Bella and the ghost disappeared in a cloud of dust.

AFTERWARDS

"Well, at least you didn't hurt yourself," said Mum, staring around glumly at her wrecked bedroom. She picked a lump of ceiling plaster off her dressing table and dropped it into the bin.

Bella had crashed through the attic floor into Mum and Dad's bedroom and landed on their king-size bed.

They'd rushed upstairs to find her in a room full of rubble and Magda and Sid's horrified faces peering down at them from a hole in the ceiling.

Once they were all safely down, Mum said, "What were you doing up there in the first place?"

"We were on a ghost hunt," explained Magda. "Bella said there was one in your attic."

"I think you found it!" said Dad, trying to catch the panicked, flapping bird that was beating itself against the window.

"Here's your ghost."

The bird took refuge on the curtain pole, glared at them all and did a big splat on the window.

Bella couldn't believe she'd thought it was a ghost. It had seemed huge in the dark, confined attic but now she could see it wasn't that big after all.

"Just some poor seabird that's lost its way," said Dad. He opened the window and the bird flew off.

"Magda was really scared!" piped up Sid.

"No I wasn't!" said Magda, her cheeks scarlet.

"Yes you were," insisted Sid. "You were screaming."

"Why didn't you come down if you didn't

like it?" asked Mum, kindly.

"I couldn't," explained Magda. "Bella had locked me in."

Mum's jaw dropped open. "Bella, you and I need to have a serious talk."

So after Magda had gone home, they did. Well, Mum talked – Bella and Sid listened.

It was all about TRUST and DOING AS YOU'RE TOLD and BEING KIND TO YOUR FRIENDS.

Bella couldn't get a word in edgeways.

At last Mum stopped talking seriously and her voice grew soft again. "You've always been such a good girl, Bella. I know you don't like living here but you mustn't take it out on poor Magda."

Bella blinked in surprise. "But I do! Like living here, I mean. I love it. I didn't mean to lock us in the attic. The door slammed shut behind me."

"And Bella *is* kind to Magda," protested Sid. "She tried to save her from the ghost. I mean the bird. But she *thought* it was a ghost!"

"That was brave of you," said Mum, and Bella smiled and stood up tall.

"Poor Magda," sighed Mum. "I'm afraid she's a bit of a trouble magnet. She seems to attract trouble wherever she goes."

"It's all right, Mum," said Sid. "She's

got our Bella to look after her now."

"*That*," said Mum, "is exactly what worries me."

READ BELLA AND MAGDA'S
NEXT ADVENTURE IN

TROUBLE
AT
SCHOOL

COMING AUGUST 2017

CHRIS HIGGINS began writing
young fiction when she rapidly acquired
a whole bunch of grandchildren, and is
the author of the *My Funny Family* series.
Chris has travelled the world and lives in
Cornwall with her husband.
Trouble Next Door is the first book in her
exciting new series for Bloomsbury.

EMILY MACKENZIE

is an illustrator and keen knitter.

She is the author and illustrator of

Wanted! Ralfy Rabbit, Book Burglar and

Stanley the Amazing Knitting Cat.

Emily lives in Edinburgh.